KT-478-416

Withdrawn from stock

SEAN TAYLOR is a children's writer, storyteller and teacher.
His books for Frances Lincoln include the Purple Class series,
The Great Snake, *The Grizzly Bear with the Frizzly Hair* and
Crocodiles are the Best Animals of All, which, along with
Purple Class and the Half-Eaten Sweater, was shortlisted for
the Roald Dahl Funny Prize 2009.
Sean lives partly in England and partly in Brazil,
with his wife and two young children.
www.seantaylorstories.com

HANNAH SHAW has written and illustrated many critically
acclaimed picture books. These include *Crocodiles are the Best Animals of All*
and *The Grizzly Bear with the Frizzly Hair* with Sean Taylor,
and *Evil Weasel*, *Erroll* and *School for Bandits*, which she wrote and illustrated.
Hannah lives in Gloucestershire with Ben the blacksmith
and Ren the dog. For details of her workshops for schools
and libraries, visit her website on
www.hannahshawillustrator.co.uk

700040343611

To Sebastião – *ST*
To Isaac – *HS*

JANETTA OTTER-BARRY BOOKS

Who Ate Auntie Iris? copyright © Frances Lincoln Limited 2012
Text copyright © Sean Taylor 2012
Illustrations copyright © Hannah Shaw 2012
The right of Sean Taylor and Hannah Shaw to be identified respectively
as the author and illustrator of this work has been asserted by them in
accordance with the Copyright, Designs and Patents Act, 1988 (United Kingdom).

First published in Great Britain and in the USA in 2012 by
Frances Lincoln Children's Books, 4 Torriano Mews,
Torriano Avenue, London NW5 2RZ
www.franceslincoln.com

This paperback edition published in Great Britain in 2012

All rights reserved

No part of this publication may be reproduced, stored in a retrieval
system, or transmitted, in any form, or by any means, electrical,
mechanical, photocopying, recording or otherwise without
the prior written permission of the publisher or a licence
permitting restricted copying. In the United Kingdom
such licences are issued by the Copyright Licensing
Agency, Saffron House, 6-10 Kirby Street,
London EC1N 8TS.

A catalogue record for this book is available
from the British Library.

ISBN 978-1-84780-314-6

Illustrated with pen and ink and scanned textures
Set in IM FELL DW Pica

Printed in Shenzhen, Guangdong, China by C&C Offset Printing in January 2012
9 8 7 6 5 4 3 2 1

Who Ate Auntie Iris?

By
SEAN TAYLOR

illustrated by
HANNAH SHAW

F
FRANCES LINCOLN
CHILDREN'S BOOKS

Look where Auntie Iris lives.

She's my favourite aunt.
And sometimes my mum brings me over
to spend the afternoon with her.
But Mum says, "My nose twitches every time
I get here. And when a chinchilla's nose
twitches it means there's danger in the air!"

Auntie Iris just smiles and tells us,
"There's no need at all to worry!"
But she does climb up the stairs
in quite a bit of a hurry.

After all, on the FIRST floor
there's a family of bears.
And every time we go past their flat
they give us
HARD BEAR STARES!

On the SECOND floor,
there's this crocodile.
And I think there's something a bit
TOO FRIENDLY
about his toothy smile.

Then on the THIRD floor,
there's a whole lot of WOLVES.
And every time they look at us
one of them always DROOLS!

Luckily no one at all
lives on the FOURTH floor.
So it feels safe from there up to
Auntie Iris's door.

Or at least it DID...

until last Thursday afternoon.
Because Auntie Iris went down
to put the rubbish out,

AND SHE
DIDN'T
COME
BACK!

I looked outside.
ALL I SAW
WAS
HER
HAT!

I crept down the stairs...
NOT A SIGN OF HER!

And it seemed pretty definite to me...

that someone had
EATEN
AUNTIE IRIS!

I had to find out who'd done it.
So I went to the first floor.
And, although my nose
was twitching with worry,
I gave a tap on the door.

Next thing it opened wide,
and a bear looked out.
I said to him,
"WHO ATE AUNTIE IRIS?"
The bear gave a scratch of his snout.

"It wasn't us," he replied.
"We're all sitting watching TV.
It's our favourite cookery programme today.
We watch it every week."

He seemed to be telling the truth.
So I went to the SECOND floor.
I didn't like the thought of those teeth,
but I gave a knock on the door.

Next thing it opened up
and there was the crocodile.
I said to him,
"WHO ATE AUNTIE IRIS?"
He gave me a friendly smile.

The 2 Swamp

"It wasn't me," he replied,
"and I'm sorry, you'll have to excuse me.
Some friends have come round to help me
install a brand-new jacuzzi."

He seemed to be telling the truth.
So I went to the third floor.
I knew that it must have been those wolves,
and I banged quite hard on their door.

One of them opened it up,
but only a little bit.
I asked him,
"WHO ATE AUNTIE IRIS?"
The wolf gave his lips a lick.

He said, "Who ate your auntie?"
Not us! We hardly know her!
We're all of us having a quiet time in,
and practising some YOGA."

He seemed to be telling the truth too.
So what was I meant to do?

AND WHO ATE AUNTIE IRIS?

I carried on up the stairs, thinking,

Was it THE WOLVES?

Was it THE CROCODILE?

Was it THE BEARS?

But then I heard a voice.
It said, "Ah! So there's my hat!
It was Auntie Iris.
SHE WAS ALL RIGHT!

"I thought someone had eaten you!" I said.
"Oh no!" she smiled back.
"I just bumped into my new neighbours,
and they showed me around their flat."

She led me back up the stairs.
I asked, "Are the new neighbours OK?"
Auntie Iris said,
"They're LIONS!"

I turned round...they were looking our way.

"Chinchillas for neighbours!" said a lion.
"I can't say how happy we feel!
We'd very much like to ask you round,
AND HAVE YOU ALL FOR A MEAL!"

Auntie Iris just smiled and told me,
"There's no need at all to worry!"
But she did climb up the stairs
in quite a bit of a hurry.

MORE GREAT PICTURE BOOKS BY SEAN TAYLOR AND HANNAH SHAW

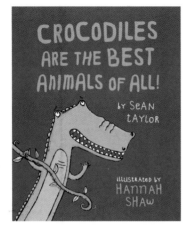

CROCODILES ARE THE BEST ANIMALS OF ALL
Sean Taylor
Illustrated by Hannah Shaw

Their ears may wiggle
And their teeth may be wonky,
But nothing is better than being a donkey.
Is it true? There's a crocodile who doesn't agree!

Shortlisted for the Roald Dahl Funny Prize 2009

"Picture book of the season." *Bookseller*

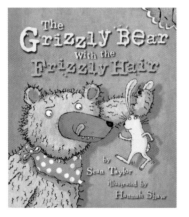

THE GRIZZLY BEAR WITH THE FRIZZLY HAIR
Sean Taylor
Illustrated by Hannah Shaw

There was nothing left to eat in the woods.
The Grizzly Bear with the Frizzly Hair had eaten it all.
And that's why he was looking bad-tempered and hungry.
That's why he was on the prowl….
So how do you think this itzy-bitzy rabbit felt
when they came face to face?

NUMBER RHYMES: *Tens and Teens*
Opal Dunn
Illustrated by Hannah Shaw

Five little monkeys; twelve fat sausages sizzling in the pan;
twenty green bottles on a wall; 100 bees round a hive….
Lots of rhymes to help develop numeracy skills, including
counting in twos, counting backwards, counting up to 20,
and in tens to 100. Numbers have never been such fun –
with wonderful, comic illustrations.

Frances Lincoln titles are available from all good bookshops.
You can also buy books and find out more about your favourite titles,
authors and illustrators on our website: www.franceslincoln.com